THE THREE
LITTLE RIGS

Written and Illustrated by

DAVID GORDON

LAURA GERINGER BOOKS
An Imprint of HarperCollinsPublishers

The Three Little Rigs   Copyright © 2005 by David Gordon
Manufactured in China by South China Printing Company Ltd.
All rights reserved.   www.harperchildrens.com
Library of Congress Cataloging-in-Publication Data   Gordon, David, date.
The three little rigs / written and illustrated by David Gordon.— 1st ed.   p.   cm.
Summary: Three little rigs look for help when the big,
bad wrecking ball comes to destroy their garages.
ISBN 0-06-058118-2 — ISBN 0-06-058119-0 (lib. bdg.)
[1. Trucks—Fiction. 2. Brothers—Fiction.] I. Title.   PZ7.G6547Th 2005
2004006170   [E]—dc22   CIP   AC
Typography by Alicia Mikles   1 2 3 4 5 6 7 8 9 10   ❖   First Edition

For Susan

A very special thanks to Nina Rappaport. Also thanks to Laura Geringer,
Tammy Shannon, Tamar Brazis, Jill Santopolo, and Alicia Mikles.

There once were three little rigs who lived
with their mama rig. She told them that the time had come for them
to go out into the world and build their own garages.

The first little rig went to the sawmill. He asked the loader for enough wood to build a sturdy garage.

"Make sure to use lots of nails!" the loader said.

The first little rig used his crane to place the wooden planks. With the help of an air compressor and a nail gun, he made four walls, a roof, and a door.

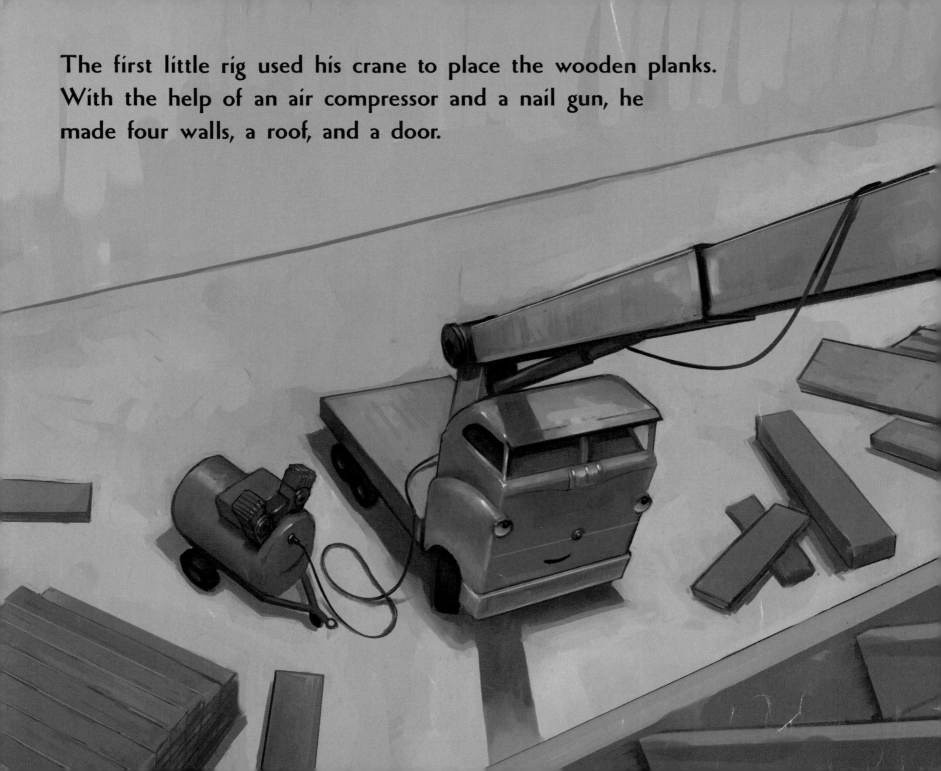

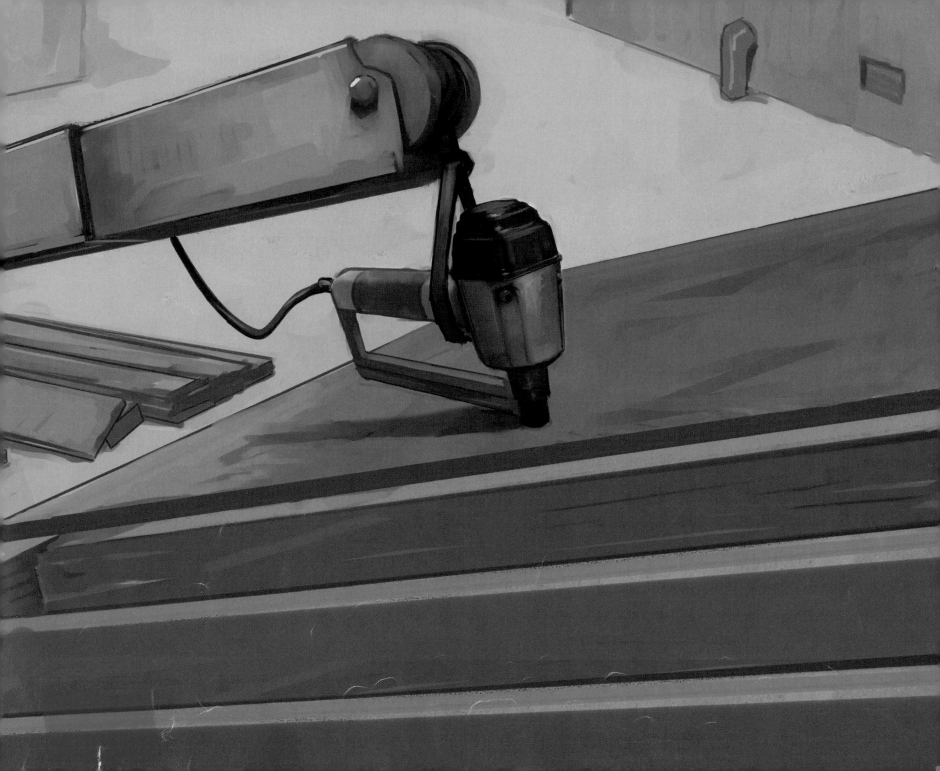

But the big, bad wrecking ball knocked on his door and said,
"Little rig, little rig, let me come in!"
To which the little rig replied, "Not by the chrome on my chinny chin chin."
This made the wrecking ball mad, so he said,
"Then I'll crash and I'll bash and I'll smash your house in."
"You just try," said the little rig.

So the wrecking ball crashed and he bashed and he smashed the garage to pieces.

The second little rig went to the stone-cutting factory. He asked the conveyor for enough blocks to build a sturdy garage. "Make sure to use enough mortar," the conveyor said.

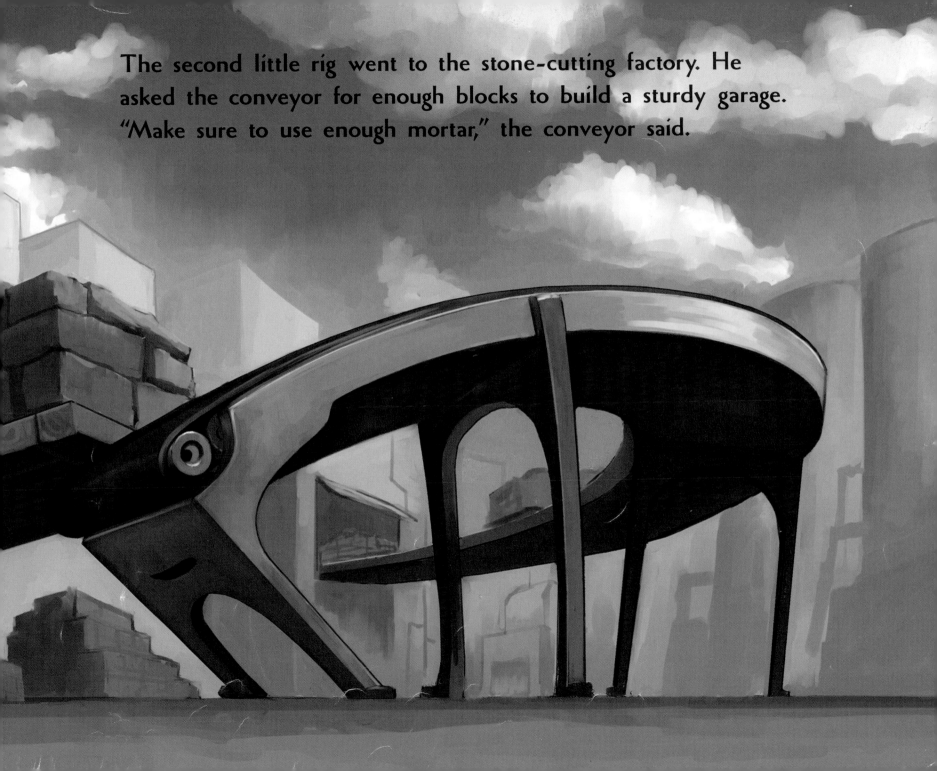

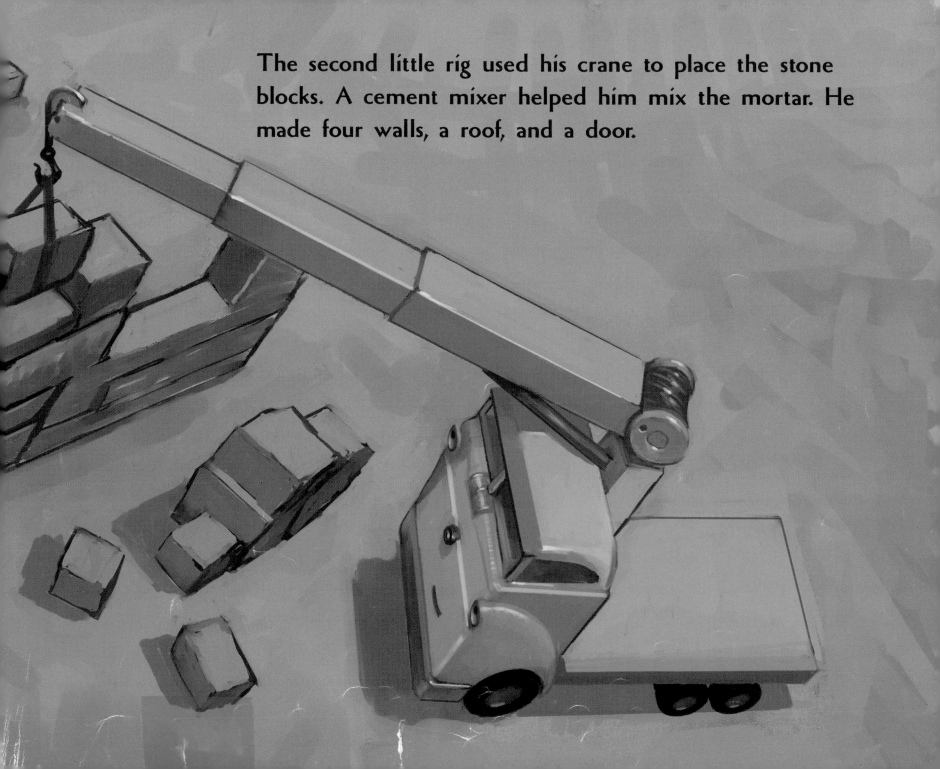

The second little rig used his crane to place the stone blocks. A cement mixer helped him mix the mortar. He made four walls, a roof, and a door.

But the big, bad wrecking ball knocked on his door and said,
"Little rig, little rig, let me come in!"
To which the little rig replied, "Not by the chrome on my chinny chin chin."
This made the wrecking ball mad, so he said,
"Then I'll crash and I'll bash and I'll smash your house in."
"You just try," said the little rig.

So the wrecking ball crashed and he bashed
and he smashed the garage to pieces.

The third little rig went to the steel mill. He asked the pulley for enough beams to build a sturdy garage.
"Make good welds," the pulley said.

The third little rig used his crane to place the steel beams. A welder helped him.

But the big, bad wrecking ball knocked on his door and said,
"Little rig, little rig, let me come in!"
To which the little rig replied, "Not by the chrome on my chinny chin chin."
This made the wrecking ball mad, so he said,
"Then I'll crash and I'll bash and I'll smash your house in."
"You just try," said the little rig.

So the wrecking ball crashed and he bashed and he crashed and he bashed, but he couldn't smash the garage to pieces.
"I'll be back," said the big, bad wrecking ball.

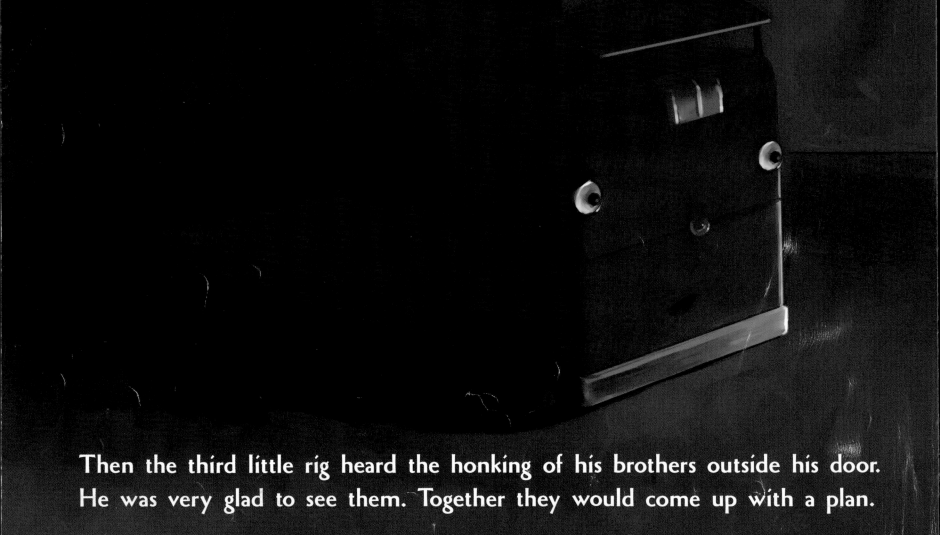

Then the third little rig heard the honking of his brothers outside his door.
He was very glad to see them. Together they would come up with a plan.

Later that night the big, bad wrecking ball returned
with the mean magnet and the cruel cutter.
"Little rig, little rig, let us come in!" they said.
To which the three little rigs replied,
"Not by the chrome on our chinny chin chins."

"Then we'll crash and we'll bash and we'll smash your house in."

"Wait!" shouted the third little rig, as his brothers snuck out the back door.

"Save us!" they cried to the cranes.

The wrecking ball began to swing. The magnet began to pull.
And the cutter began to cut at the third little rig's garage.
Suddenly the cranes lifted the dangerous three high into the air!

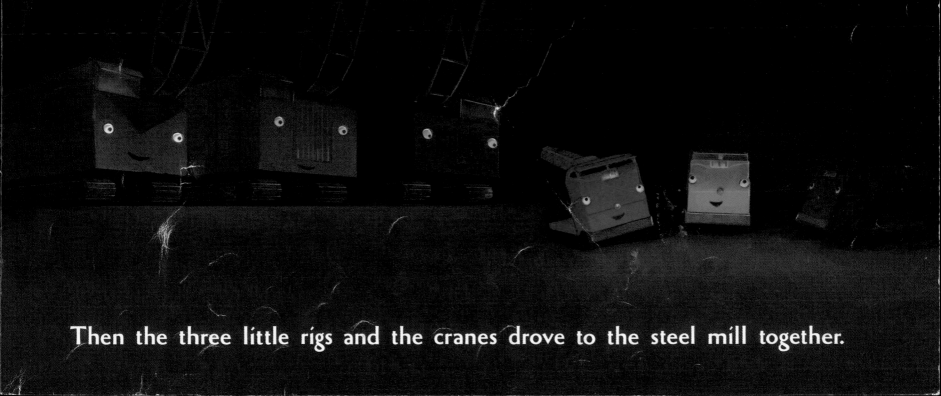

Then the three little rigs and the cranes drove to the steel mill together.

There the big, bad wrecking ball,
the mean magnet, and the cruel cutter
were thrown into the melting pot.

And the three little rigs all lived happily ever after.